GOODNIGHT GOODNIGHT

Brenda Parkes

Illustrated by
Terry Denton

For Emma.

I love to read
in bed at night.
Then Teddy and I
turn out the light.

And as we dream
the night away,
our story book friends
come out to play.

Who's that looking in my cupboard? It's my friend, Old ...

Mother Hubbard.

Jump on my bed
and join the fun.

**There's lots of room
for everyone!**

Who's that climbing up the stairs?

It's Goldilocks and ...

The Three Bears.

Jump on my bed
and join the fun.

**There's lots of room
for everyone!**

Who's that running as fast as he can?

You can't catch him.
He's the ...

Jump on my bed
and join the fun.

There's lots of room for *everyone!*

Fee Fi Fo Fum.
Can you guess
who's next to come?

Let's all pull
the curtain back ...

It's Jack!

*Jump on my bed
and join the fun.*

***There's lots of room
for everyone!***

Sometimes we have a pillow fight.

Sometimes we give a bear a frigh

Sometimes we read, all snuggled tigh

And now it's morning.
It's getting light.

I wonder who will come tonight.